TEDD ARNOLD

HUGGLY
TAKES A BATH

SCHOLASTIC INC. Cartwheel ·B·O·O·K·S·®

New York   Toronto   London   Auckland   Sydney

Look for Huggly in Scholastic's  **CD-ROM**

Copyright © 1998 by Tedd Arnold.
All rights reserved. Published by Scholastic Inc.
HUGGLY and THE MONSTER UNDER THE BED are trademarks of Tedd Arnold. CARTWHEEL BOOKS and the CARTWHEEL BOOKS logo are trademarks and/or registered trademarks of Scholastic Inc.

Library of Congress Cataloging-in-Publication Data

Arnold, Tedd.
    Huggly takes a bath/ by Tedd Arnold.
       p.   cm. — (Monster under the bed)
    "Cartwheel books."
    Summary: When he ventures out from under the bed one night, Huggly tries to figure out the use for various items in the bathroom.
    ISBN 0-590-11760-2
    [1. Bathrooms — Fiction.   2. Monsters — Fiction.]   I. Title.   II. Series.
PZ7.A7379Hw   1998
[E] — dc21

97-21414
CIP
AC

10 9

8 9/9 0/0 01 02

Printed in the U.S.A.   24
First printing, February 1998

It was dark and quiet in the house...
time to explore.

But Huggly didn't want to wake the people child on the bed!

Huggly wondered about the one room with a light on.

"Maybe there are snacks in here," he thought.

He squished some green goop out of a tube. "Not bad," he said.

He found some pink stuff in a dish. "Yuck!"

Huggly found
tiny brushes...

a big bowl with
a lid...

and a huge tub.

Huggly climbed onto the side of the tub.

He slid in. "Whee! This is fun!" he said.

His foot kicked something. Water! He
kicked the other something. More water!
But the water went down a hole.

Huggly plugged the hole. The tub filled with water.

"This is okay," he said, "but not as nice as my slime pit back home."

"What's this?" He opened a bottle.
Slimy stuff. He dumped it into the
water.

"Wow! Bubbles!" He laughed.
"This must be magic slime."

He emptied more bottles of slime
into the water.

"This is the best slime pit ever!" he said.

When Huggly finally climbed out of the
slime pit, he was covered with bubbles.

He shaped the bubbles with his hands. "Hey, look! I'm a snow monster!"

"Now I'm a dragon."

"Now I'm a ghost!"

Suddenly the door opened and the
people child walked to the big bowl.

"Yikes!" Huggly jumped over the child and raced out the door.

The people father hurried into the room.
"What's all the racket about?" the father asked.

"Wait, let me guess. A monster from under the bed gave you a bath?"

"No," said the child. "It was a fluffy white ghost."